Mischief in Moonstone Series, Novella 5: A Moonstone Wedding

By Christine DeSmet

Writers Exchange E-Publishing
http://www.writers-exchange.com

Chapter 1

Margie Mueller's life was about to crash like two logging trucks that missed the elbow-shaped curve outside of Moonstone in the Northwoods of Wisconsin. She had to tell Tony Farina their wedding was off. Her heart stung from the surprise gift he'd had delivered to her trailer that steamy, August morning.

By late that Thursday afternoon, she couldn't eat, unusual for Margie. Her four girlfriends taste-tested wedding reception food in the Jingle Bell Inn restaurant, a restored dining room of the mansion dubbed the North Pole. For a moment they were distracted from the savory cheddar cheese-topped potatoes by the view out the large windows. Two bare-chested, bronzed men pounded with hammers under the sun. They were finishing the deck surrounding the new, four-season glass room. It had a breathtaking view of Lake Superior.

Even Chef Kirsten Van Brocklin paused in her hurry back and forth between their usual corner table and the kitchen. "It's just not fair that we're already married."

"But," said petite Lily Bauer, the bank teller, who fingered her pearl necklace, "we can look at the menu as long as we don't order. Now's your last chance, Margie, to catch a little nooky with Dustin and Casey before you get married."

Margie's gaze skated over the carpenters to the lake. Slanting sunlight painted the crests of rolling waves pink--Margie's favorite color. But Margie was not feeling "in the pink". Margie felt blue, nervous about every aspect of her life right now, embarrassed.

She picked at the cranberry-and-rice-stuffed pork chops in a sauce made with pear wine from a nearby Bayfield winery. She poked at her favorite salad--strawberry gelatin with pink marshmallows folded in. This salad had been shaped like a fish in an aluminum mold. Strawberry slices created the fish's scales. The pink marshmallow eyes seemed to taunt Margie about Tony's betrayal.

Jeri Kaminski, a leggy, sinewy blonde who drove a school bus, plunked down her fork. "What's wrong? This frothy fish fluff is gonna impress the heck out of Tony's relatives."

The women chattered about Margie's brilliant idea of using retro aluminum molds in wildlife shapes for the wedding fare.

Margie tried to make her announcement. "Tony and I are like Jack Sprat who could eat no fat and his wife who could eat no lean. We're ridiculous together."

Rita Johnson, who ran the post office, raised a forkful of gelatin in toast. "Tony says you're voluptuous, his Sophia Loren."

Lily said, "He loves curves, Margie. Maybe it has something to do with him being a chef on a boat, riding all those swells and swales and shallows and shoals."

The women glanced from Lily fingering the pearls around her skinny neck to the men outdoors. Margie would need three times the pearls for her own neck. She would hang herself with them. That would be better than confronting Tony about that morning's delivery.

"Tony is sexier than both those guys combined," Jeri said. "And you're just as sexy. It was your 42-Ds and that bikini trick we pulled that lured Tony in the first place."

A year ago, after they discovered the men lied about fishing and had started taking nightly cruises on a party boat featuring topless waitresses, the friends hatched the plan to wear almost nothing to their jobs. Tony, the boat's chef, shopped at Margie's IGA grocery and fell in love with her sexy curves on display in a bikini at the checkout counter.

Margie had tried hard to make the relationship work. She dyed her mousey, graying hair to auburn and grew it shoulder length. "Tony's family will know I'm trying to snag him out of desperation before I hit my big Five-O."

The gamine Felicity scoffed, her dark eyes and cap of black hair sleek with youth. "Look at Henri and me, over fifty years apart in age. Fifty is a lucky number. We even had a baby." The former nun had married eighty-some Henri LeBarron, the town's Santa Claus and owner of the North Pole mansion. "It'll work out."

Margie choked into her napkin. "But Tony deserves babies. He's just not thinking clearly about my age."

Jeri asked, "Babies? Tony's what? Fifty-something?"

"Forty-nine. A few months younger than I am," Margie said. "He needs a younger wife."

Felicity said, "Whatever for? A brood mare? What's really bothering you?"

"I bring nothing to that family. I'm a Lutheran German who likes sauerkraut, church pancake suppers, and Jell-o." She honked into her napkin. "My family consists of a loud-mouth, farmer brother I haven't seen in years. I'll end up being the Farina's 'funny' aunt."

Lily said, "You're suffering from cold feet." She handed her pearls over. "Something borrowed, for your wedding."

"They won't fit."

Jeri said, "Rita's husband sells extensions over at the hardware store."

Rita nodded, her mouth full of another Margie favorite: a bacon-wrapped mushroom that had been simmered in beer, stuffed with local wild rice and goat cheese, then browned. "Yummy. Don't change a thing. And don't change a thing about you, Margie. His family will love you. When are they coming, by the way?"

Margie groaned. "In a couple of days." They'd arrive on Saturday, in time for Sunday's bridal shower and Tony's bachelor party, then stay a week until the wedding the following Saturday. Margie had to cancel the wedding before they got on airplanes.

Kirsten showed up with the wedding cake sample, chocolate with pink marshmallow frosting whipped to look like the lake's waves. "This'll be in tiers with chocolate bears on top dressed like a bride and groom. Tell me, Margie, if it's sweet enough to please Tony's mom."

Margie's eyes burned with tears. Tony adored his mother. He emailed her every day.

Lily dug into the pink fluff. "Where are all those relatives from Italy staying? How many are coming?"

Pent-up anxiety gave way. Margie bawled into her napkin. "I can't marry Tony."

Kirsten put a hand on her shoulder. "What's wrong, honey?"

"He wants children. He's changed his mind. Our dream was to have him find jobs on cruise ships and we'd travel the world. But he lied."

Lily licked frosting off her finger. "When did he say this?"

"He didn't exactly say it, but he had a fertility rug delivered to me this morning, all the way from Italy."

"A fertility rug?!" the women screeched. "What's that?"

"It's a red rug, woven with birds making nests."

Kirsten pulled up a chair. "How do you know it's a big fat hint to have kids?"

"It had a note from Tony's mom. 'For good fortune and family, for good luck at your blessed event. Love, Antoinette.' Felicity, is it some Catholic thing?"

"Priests bless farms for good yields," Felicity said. "I suppose you can sprinkle holy water on a rug."

Margie stared at her uneaten cake. "So it's real. Tony had his mother send a baby-making rug."

Felicity asked, "How big is this rug?"

"Maybe six by twelve feet."

"It's likely one of those things where everybody stands on it and holds hands in a circle while you and Tony kiss."

"While they chant about babies." Margie moaned.

Kirsten said, "I think that's voodoo where they chant."

Felicity laughed. "Margie, have you talked about this with Father Joe?"

"He's hard of hearing. I don't want to shout, 'We're calling off the wedding because of a sex rug.'"

Jeri said, "Leave the darn thing rolled up in a corner. Where are they staying, anyway?"

A hot flash whooshed up Margie's face. "Nowhere. I can't find hotel rooms for two dozen people. Everything's booked in Superior and Duluth for a deer hunters' show."

Rita said, "So we'll each take in a couple, and several could stay with Alyssa and John at that big house they've been refurbishing."

"It's haunted, remember," Margie choked out. "Tony's mother believes in the Holy Ghost, not ghosts."

The women relived how their friend Alyssa Swain discovered true love and ghosts of dead relatives in her house last Halloween. The pleasant recollection made Margie want to evaporate into the woodwork, too.

Rita said, "Have them stay on the tour boat. My husband sells air mattresses."

Margie said, "It's booked next week. Tony has to work the lunches."

"Work?" Kirsten shook her head in disbelief. "He hired an assistant chef who should be able to take over. Cute guy."

"Giovanni Casale. Tony knew his family in Chicago. But Gio just graduated from tech school. Tony says he needs a lot of training yet."

Lily said, "Surely Tony's not spending all his time with Gio. That's not why you're upset, is it?"

Margie blinked back tears. "Tony comes over to my trailer regularly, despite Herman."

Lily gasped. "Herman doesn't watch, does he?"

Herman was Margie's Saint Bernard dog. "Of course not. But he barks when we're on the floor kissing or whatever. I think he thinks we're moaning in pain." She burned with embarrassment. "Tony likes to use the whole house..."

Jeri asked, "You have sex in a different room every night?"

"But it's only a trailer. Only two rooms--main open living area and the bedroom. Tony's getting bored. He must be or he wouldn't have okayed the fertility rug."

Felicity slapped the table. "Let's switch. You and the Farinas move in here in the mansion, and Henri and I will take your trailer for a week. Tony will have three stories of rooms for sex plus the wine cellar."

Margie's heart pounded like a dryer with a shoe in it. "But what about all your antiques? What if the Steuben glass collection gets broken or the tables get scratched?"

Lily cooed, "I'll keep the Steubens. That leaping glass fish is phallic. It'll put my husband in the mood."

Jeri said, "Dibs on the red Chinese vase. Hubby becomes a bull around red."

"Whoa." Felicity held up a hand. "Margie needs to impress his family."

"But it's not my house."

"But your idea," Felicity said. "Have Tony tell them he rented it at your suggestion."

Kirsten clapped. "Live rich. And you have a built-in chef--me."

Jeri said, "I'll come by in my school bus to take the relatives out to Tootsie Winters' farm to see her lavender silkie chickens."

Tootsie's husband, Bob, used to run Moonstone. The former mayor now managed the tour boat that Tony worked on.

Margie's stomach tightened. "Thanks, but--"

Felicity smiled. "It's done. A perfect solution."

A perfect disaster, Margie thought.

Chapter 2

On Friday, Tony and Margie had a whole day alone at the North Pole.

It was a day of sublime small talk, of kisses, of cabernet and cheese, and appreciation of the delicate Steuben animals in their surroundings. Every small nicety made Margie more nervous. Tony was too perfect for her. She had cold feet and her feet felt as fragile as those on the glass creatures.

At one point, Tony took Margie's face in his palms, his brown eyes almost ebony with passion. "My beautiful Margaret, more beautiful than Sophia Loren, what is the one thing my angel wants from life? I'll get it for you."

In the past she'd said things like Liz Taylor perfume, a case of German Hofbrau beer, and a new Green Bay Packer collar for Herman. This time she needed to say, "Let me out of this marriage," but instead red licorice popped into her head and out of her mouth. "I haven't had that since I was a girl."

Tony pressed spicy kisses from her lips to her toes. His fervor made it hard to talk to Tony about the so-called fertility rug.

Prior to Tony's family arriving from Italy, Margie's friends came early Saturday to make beds, bring in pink roses, and perfume the dresser drawers. They moved Margie to the third floor of the mansion. Tony would stay on the second floor across from his parents. Because the second floor parlor would host the bridal shower, the women dusted the Steuben collection and everything to white-glove perfection.

The fertility carpet stayed in its long box in the foyer. Tony hadn't even asked about it. Margie suspected he wanted to wait until his mother arrived from Italy, which made her more miserable.

Father Joe arrived in the mid-afternoon. He was a retired priest from Illinois who made Moonstone his summer home. Standing in the foyer, the shrunken man with white hair looked up at her with gentle blue eyes. "My dear, you are blessed to have found Tony Farina."

Margie sidled up to her dreaded topic. "Has Tony talked with you about, well, us?"

"I'm very well, thank you."

She tried again, louder. "Have you talked about us as a couple?"

"I reassured Tony that you're lovely. He says you're strong and perfect for him."

Margie frowned. "I'm strong? For what?"

"Tony needs someone who can be a good mother."

"A mother?" *This is horrible.* "He talked with you about my being a mother?"

Father Joe took one of her hands in his bony clasp. "My dear, he's always had strong women in his life. He wants to please his mother. He sees you as pleasing her."

"In what way?" *As a brood mare?*

"Tony needs you to care for him, to give all of yourself."

Margie was even more confused. "To give myself how?" *Children?*

"My dear, I believe you have company."

The doorbell rang a second time. Heat needled her face. *Swell. I'm beet red and I itch, just in time to meet my future in-laws. Or will they be my in-laws? Why am I so scared? Does every bride-to-be who's not sure have this kind of scrambled brain and tied tongue?* She smoothed her pink, short-sleeved blouse and clam-digger pants, took a deep breath, then opened the door.

Air redolent with pines and new-mown lawn swirled in along with the floral perfume of Antoinette Farina. Bejeweled combs in her bountiful black hair matched her red satin blouse worn with cream-colored silk pants. The family filed in forever in a long line behind her. Tony and Father Joe shook their hands and kissed their cheeks.

Margie was taken aback when a handsome guy of maybe twenty-five came through the door doing karate moves that ended with flipping Tony on the floor. Margie hurried over. "Are you all right?"

Antoinette gave the karate expert a slap upside the head. "Did you not sit in jail for this behavior?"

Tony brushed off his white shirt and introduced Margie to his cousin, Nico. "He's still single. Now you know why."

Nico laughed, hanging an elbow on Tony's shoulder. "I may not be single for long if all the women of Moonstone look like this. I'll slay dragons for you, baby."

Antoinette wailed, "Slaying is not a joke. Dom, do something about your nephew."

Domenico Farina and the clan erupted into arguments about Nico running with the wrong crowd and getting somebody killed but it was his own fault, not Nico's.

Herman barked and barked, his tail slapping hips and thighs.

As quickly as the fracas had crescendoed, it decrescendoed into introductions. Tony was the oldest of four sons and two daughters. The family in the foyer included husbands, wives, children, teenagers, cousins, plus widowed Aunt Alberta--Tony's mother's sister.

Curly-haired, six-year-old twins Renzo and Romeo rode Herman down a hallway. Margie cringed when they jiggled a table that held a priceless vase.

Tony's father, a tall man with steel gray hair, cradled Margie's hand between his warm palms. "As my Tony informed me, you are more beautiful than Sophia Loren. And my son has found a castle for his wedding week befitting of the Farina name. My son, I am proud. I look forward to hearing more about the villa you will build your beautiful bride."

Amid cheers, Tony's brothers lifted Tony off his feet and carried him in a circle. When they set him down, Nico gave him a friendly punch in the gut. Margie winced.

Tony obviously hadn't told his family that he and Margie would live in her one-bedroom, pink trailer on the edge of town. What else hadn't Tony told them? That was answered when Antoinette ordered her sons to open the long box and unfurl the red rug.

Margie held her breath. She looked across the birds' nests at Tony. He smiled like a drunk--a man drunk on his family.

Antoinette clasped her hands over her heart. "Every one of my precious children has taken their vows on this fertility carpet."

Nico punched Tony's shoulder. Tony looked away. Margie's heartbeat down-shifted into disappointment.

To her relief, Father Joe asked about the location of the ceremony. That sent the clan outdoors for a tour.

Margie excused herself to check on food preparations. And to hide.

On her way down the hallway toward the restaurant she ran into Renzo, Romeo, and Herman. The boys slammed into her legs. She'd never had a leg hug before.

"I love your dog."

"And you'd be?"

"I'm Renzo." He wore a red shirt.

The other one wore purple. She said, "And you must be Romeo."

"Yeth!" Romeo had lost his front teeth. "Can we have cookieth?"

"If your mom says okay."

"You're pretty."

Romeo lived up to his name. She ruffled his curly mop. "How about taking Herman outside?"

The boys screeched so loud it hurt Margie's ears. Herman's barking was as bad. Romeo climbed on the dog while Renzo caught Herman's wagging tail.

She settled with her bridal shower menu in her usual, *quiet* corner. The restaurant would fill soon. The early-bird specials started at four, in an hour. She smelled bread baking. The odor should have calmed her, but she fizzed with the fear that her impending marriage was a mistake.

To her chagrin, Antoinette came in and seated herself. "May I, if it is of course a good time for you, for me to get to know you?"

Antoinette's politeness struck Margie with more terror. "Sure. I'm just going over tomorrow's party menu."

Antoinette sniffed the air and smiled. She wore a giant red gem that matched her satin blouse--and that darn rug. Margie glanced down at her own pink, discount store duds. Maybe Antoinette already saw the mismatch and would call off the wedding, saving Margie the task.

The regal woman glanced into the new glass room. Dustin and Casey were installing white floor tiles. "My son tells me this is an aviary. There will be birds? Would that not be a mess?"

"The birds won't be loose to poop on stuff." A scene of birds dive-bombing the Farinas played in Margie's head. "Peter LeBarron loves exotic birds. He and his father Henri own this place. The birds will be caged among tropical plants far from the tables. Peter says they have stuff like that at resorts around the world."

"What resorts do you prefer? My family has found splendid ones in Chile."

Margie felt as if she stood on marsh muck and was sinking rapidly. "I've never been outside the country. But I've been to Vegas. There's a casino called Paris. Did you know there's a Paris, Texas? And a Paris, Missouri, Arizona, Illinois, Kentucky, and Tennessee? I haven't been to any of them, but wouldn't that make a cool RV trip?"

After a blank stare, Antoinette asked, "What will you serve your wedding guests?"

Margie excelled at one thing--helping people at her grocery store decide what to eat for supper. "We'll have pork chops with cranberry stuffing, celery sticks with strawberry cream cheese and a Tater Tot casserole, too, because--" *It has special meaning for Tony and me.* "Because everybody likes it. And Tony's asked a cheese factory to dye their cheese curds pink for us. The curds squeak in your teeth."

Antoinette didn't move.

Margie told her about the variety of pink gelatin molds. "There'll also be Wisconsin wheat beers because their red color looks sort of pinkish. The kids'll get strawberry milk."

Antoinette gave a curt nod. "Milk is good for children."

Ever the nincompoop, Margie kept sinking into the muck. "The cake is red German chocolate made with sauerkraut. Ever tried that?"

"There is nothing of Tony's favorite foods."

The statement hit Margie like a steak knife impaling her hand onto the table. "It's the kind of food we like in Moonstone."

"To please you, I'm sure he neglected to tell you things."

Margie's mouth drained of its spit. Had she been blinded by Tony's passion? His "Tater Tots"? Margie also felt her own pride bubbling to life with this challenging woman and her family. "Tell me what Tony likes."

Antoinette folded her hands on the table. "Instead of the potatoes we could have polenta with a porcini sauce. He loves steamed clams with vermouth cream, too. As the anti pasti. I'm sure your wiggly animals are for the children. For the adults, we must have greens with arugula or radicchio, along with white beans. And I'm sure you meant for the chocolate cake to be for the children, too. You must have a white wedding cake, to express the bride's purity."

Margie forced an aching smile. "I'm blessed to have you help me."

Antoinette sighed like a satisfied cat that had just lapped up cream-- probably vermouth cream. "Will white doves be released? An orchestra hired?"

Margie squeaked, "I'm putting pink streamers and a disco ball in the aviary, and we're hiring a DJ who'll play polkas."

"The flowers?"

"I'm putting pink zinnias from my yard in quart jars that people can take home. They can use the jars for canning later."

Silence crawled about the room for a few seconds. Margie wondered again whether she'd be free to be herself in this family.

Antoinette took Margie's hands in her warm ones. "We'll find real vases. You are marrying my eldest son. This, above all weddings, must be perfect. Now, if you'll excuse me, I must talk with Father Joe."

"Why?"

"Haven't you noticed the poor man needs a hearing aid?"

"You're going to tell him to get one?"

Antoinette laughed. "I'm going over the ceremony with him. I have an ill feeling he doesn't understand we must add Tony's Aunt Alberta to the proceedings somewhere."

"We do?"

"She's a retired operatic star. Your wedding cannot be complete until Alberta shatters glass with her high notes. For good luck."

For the second time within an hour of meeting Tony's mother, Margie excused herself to run an errand. Running for Canada occurred to her, too.

Chapter 3

Margie sweated through her blouse by the time she crossed the town square and skidded into her grocery store. Swarthy Gio was talking with Margie's clerk, the equally good-looking Harris Healy. Harris was about ten years older than the young Giovanni, Margie estimated. Harris had returned to college after a hiatus to work and save money, and then he'd returned to school to finish his chef and restaurant management studies. Now, just out of college, Harris had a crush on Margie and didn't hide it.

"Hey, you still with that Tony baloney?" Harris asked, his usual greeting

"Yes," Margie puffed.

"What's wrong with my woman?"

Margie hesitated divulging too much about Tony's family in front of his assistant chef, but she couldn't help herself. "Tony's mother. I suspect she's rearranging all the furniture and bringing down the Steuben glass collection to use as wedding favors."

Gio kissed Margie's hand. "You could divorce Tony and marry me. Then I'll be filthy rich."

Harris punched Gio in the arm. "Hey, that's my idea."

Gio nodded toward the window. "Here comes Father Joe for wedding talk." Gio picked up his groceries and high-tailed it out of the store.

Harris chuckled. "He's too young. Doesn't understand true love."

Margie waved Harris aside. "Why don't you go help Gio on the cruise boat?"

Harris batted his eyelashes at her. "Instead, maybe we could polish the Steubens together?"

"Harris, give it up. I'm getting married." *Or am I?*

Father Joe toddled in and headed down an aisle.

Harris placed a hand over his heart, his focus on Margie. "Let's rob a bank, pay off the last of my college bills, run away to Mexico, live on a beach-_"

"Out!"

He winked and left. How simple eloping with Harris would be compared to enduring the chaos at the mansion and in her heart.

Father Joe came to the counter carrying an armload of germ-killing hand gel bottles.

"Father, what's all this?"

"Mrs. Farina requested a supply."

"Why?"

"She was muttering about bird poop at the wedding. I think I need to get a hearing aid."

"So that you can tune her out."

"Tuna? She wanted tuna, too? I'll be right back."

Margie sighed as the priest ambulated down an aisle.

The next day, Sunday, Margie tried to act happy at her bridal shower. Little Renzo and Romeo chased around her legs with Herman, begging her to play. She swung each of them in the air playfully and set them on Herman. He lumbered like a pony out of the parlor. When she turned around, the Farinas clapped.

Antoinette rushed to Tony. "Isn't she wonderful with children?"

Again Tony wore a crooked smile, incapacitated by motherly love.

Margie's shower gifts included family heirlooms of pewter candlesticks, a silver tea set, and forty-eight hand-painted dinner plates from Antoinette. Margie should've been touched, but as the wrapping paper piled up, Margie felt herself being buried.

Two hours later--after wine had flowed and the children were put down for a nap--Tony took her by the hand, sneaked to the attic, and made love to her.

Margie wasn't her exuberant self, though.

Tony noticed the change. "My angel, what is it you want? I'll get it for you."

Again he held her face. They exchanged souls through their eyes. She waited for Tony to tell her the truth about his feelings about the fertility rug. But he only grinned, waiting for her. She tried to form the right words...

Instead, she whispered, "Pink fingernail polish."

He chuckled. "For your sexy toes? I'll put it on for you."

He seemed awfully eager about a makeover. She peered at her chipped fingernails. "I need to gussy up for your family."

He kissed her. "Thank you. And I love the way you talk."

What did he mean by that? That he agreed she *needed* to gussy up? That she wasn't *good enough?* Should she learn *more Italian and use fewer old-fashioned terms?*

When she returned to the parlor she found it gloriously empty. She slunk to a leather chair. She stared into the empty hearth, looking for the words to tell Tony the wedding was off. She thought back to Harris's offer to elope and to help her dust the Steubens. She reached over to pick up one of the exquisite glass objects--

They were gone. Margie shot up. They weren't in the room.

Margie wandered about the mansion the rest of the day, spying into bedrooms, and cupboards. The only things she couldn't riffle through were the Farina suitcases. Had they lifted the LeBarron's priceless collection?

At bedtime, Margie found a ransom note tucked under her door.

Chapter 4

At daybreak on Monday, Margie called Harris to open the store. Then she called her girlfriends--except for Felicity LeBarron--for an early breakfast in their favorite corner. Margie couldn't bring herself to tell Felicity that her husband's expensive glass menagerie had boarded an ark-of-sorts and disappeared.

This time Tootsie Winters joined the group that included Rita, Jeri, Lily, and Margie. Kirsten took a break from the kitchen to listen to Margie's reading of the note.

It was in block letters and halting English. Margie read, "*Put fifty thousand in paper bag in field noon south village or bad stuff.*"

Kirsten took off her chef's hat. "That's a lot of dough."

Margie yelped, "Never mind that. 'Bad stuff' is going to happen!"

Tootsie tisked. "That new mother-in-law hid them to make you look bad."

Margie had thought of that, too. "The block printing is neat as a pin, like Antoinette."

Lily said, "I can get fake money from the bank. We'll deliver it and let the glass kidnapper escape. Joke's on her."

Practical Kirsten said, "I bet cousin Nico did it. He likes jokes. And isn't he the violent one who karate-chopped Tony upon arrival? Let's just ignore it."

They agreed to try that first.

In closing her store after dark that night Margie stumbled into a paper bag on the sidewalk. It clinked--with the broken Steuben fish.

A note said, "Will break one by one until money put in field."

Margie could barely sleep that night. She wondered how she'd tell Tony about this embarrassing joke that involved his relatives. This had to be Nico's doings. She recalled someone mentioned he'd killed somebody, albeit not his fault it seemed, but maybe he owed somebody after a lawsuit. It made her wonder. Could Nico kill again? Thinking he could somehow get away with it, then return to Italy untouched? A chill rippled across her. She burrowed deeper into the satin sheets.

On Tuesday, Margie called another breakfast meeting of the Moonstone Mavens. They created a list of suspects.

Kirsten served potato pancakes with raspberries on top, and brewed coffee with cinnamon sticks to wake up their deduction skills.

Margie started the conversation with her confusion and doubts about Nico. "He's part of the family. Why would he need or want fifty thousand dollars?"

The women mulled that over. Tootsie offered, "A young, handsome man might be in big trouble financially, and he doesn't want his family to know about it. My husband Bob and I have had our share of such troubles over the years."

"But you didn't destroy valuable artworks to try and solve it," Margie noted. "What if he did kill somebody in the past and now they're suing him? He needs money."

Lily fingered her pearl necklace. "That sounds like a TV show plot."

"It's not. I thought about it in bed last night."

Rita said, "Maybe it's not Nico but somebody very close to you."

Blood seemed to drain from Margie. "Not Tony!"

"I mean Harris. He's perhaps so disappointed with you marrying Tony that he wants money for his pain."

Tootsie nodded. "Punishment for your affair."

Margie flinched. "There's nothing going on between Harris and me." But she recalled her intrigue with his offer to run away to Mexico.

"An affair of the heart is as bad as actual sex," Tootsie said, her usual blunt self. "And isn't Harris still paying off some school debts? People in their thirties are desperate to get rid of debts these days."

Margie thought Tootsie was making way too much sense. She just couldn't believe her own employee would try to extort money from her. Margie huffed, "Maybe we should put your hubby, Bob, on the list. He collects antiques to display on the cruise boat. He'd know how to sell kidnapped Steuben glass."

Tootsie shrugged. "He wouldn't risk another heart attack. Kidnapping is too much excitement for him. He can barely collect eggs from my silkie chickens without fear of being pecked on a hand."

Lily offered, "Maybe it's Gio and Harris horsing around. Margie, you pointed out that they're both recent college grads, with tons of debt."

Tootsie said, "Didn't I tell you?" She looked pointedly at Margie.

"But," said Jeri, "the Steuben fish was crushed. Harris and Gio aren't mean."

Margie added, "And they're careful. There's never been a broken item in my store with Harris, and Gio is meticulous in the kitchen on the boat, Harris says. Gio is probably averse to glassware anywhere near his pots and pans, and he's neat to a fault as a cook, so I can't see him intentionally smashing glass and courting getting hurt."

Tootsie said, "Forget it. The LeBarron's insurance will pay for this, Margie."

None of them had thought about the insurance. So yet again they went about their business as usual.

Later that Tuesday at the mansion, at the final fitting of Margie's gown, Antoinette decided the pink sash and bow had to go. That made Margie wonder again if Antoinette were trying to get rid of Margie. What if Antoinette had arranged the elaborate scheme to send crushed glass and threatening notes to Margie? Tony's mother might have easily paid Nico to perform the dirty tricks. If the family were richer than rich, it may not matter to break a few expensive works of art for the sake of cancelling her son's wedding.

Margie looked at the note again. She had kept it hidden from Tony for fear it was indeed written by his mother. The person had hand-written it in neat block letters. So many kids today, too, didn't know cursive writing and printed messages in block lettering. Many a grocery list she'd seen at her IGA store was in simple printed words. This made her think of Harris. Was he so truly in love with her that he'd do this? She thought he might; her instincts said he had true amorous feelings toward her.

On Wednesday morning, Margie opened the mansion's front door to leave for the store when she almost tripped over the rolled up fertility rug. Margie suspected Antoinette had sent it out to be cleaned and it'd just been delivered. When Margie tried to move it, however, it wouldn't budge. In disbelief at her lack of strength, she tried again but dropped it with a grunt. It unfurled itself...

And kept on unwinding--

Bouncing down the steps of the veranda...

Finally landing onto the walkway where a body flopped out.

Father Joe.

Margie trotted down the steps in horror.

A very dead Father Joe had a note taped to his clerical collar. It read: *I want dead presidents or more close to you be dead.*

Margie's veins iced. She looked about. The morning fog and haze off Lake Superior filtered the sunlight and helped block the view from the street in front of the mansion. The Farinas still slept. Tony had left through the kitchen earlier.

Margie rolled up Father Joe in the rug, dragged him through the dewy grass to the side of the tall veranda and unhitched the storage door underneath the decking. She stooped, waddling and crawled at times inside the dark cave, pulling the rug inside behind her.

After crawling back out and then shutting and latching the door, she took out her cell phone and texted the Mavens.

Chapter 5

The girlfriends clutched their coffee cups. The sun now drenched the outdoors. Through the windows of the mansion's first floor restaurant alcove Margie watched the innocent little Farina boys looking for agates on the Lake Superior shoreline. A few relatives were with the boys, along with Herman who leaped about fetching a stick one of the family members threw for him. The innocent summer scene made Margie swallow hard at what she'd done early that morning.

Tootsie whispered, "What's the kidnapper mean by 'close to you'? Is Tony going to be dead next?"

Margie grabbed a nearby napkin to staunch sudden tears. "I hadn't thought of that."

Lily said, "It's my fault. I should've insisted we use the fake bills."

Rita said, "Any of the people in this mansion could've done it. There are several relatives here."

Tootsie said, "Every family has a rotten egg or two."

Margie recalled the argument between Antoinette and Nico about somebody being killed in the past and voiced that.

The women considered that a good lead.

Jeri Kaminski said, "I learned driving bus that you have to look them in the eyes. Have you looked all the relatives in the eyes? Does anybody seem shifty? Did they not make eye contact?"

Margie didn't remember. "I've been so nervous that I think I'm the one who doesn't make eye contact." She regretted the sound of that. "Do they think I'm shifty? Dishonest? Marrying Tony for his money? And why am I worrying?" She groaned. "It's not like me to be like this, so indecisive and obviously not worthy of that family."

Lily fingered her pearls. "You're allowed to feel inadequate. We all do from time to time. We're here for you."

Tootsie nodded toward the window where the carpenters had begun pounding on the new gazebo and benches. "What about Dustin and Casey? They could use the money. And have you seen how carpenters write on their bills they give you? They don't take the time for full sentences. And they print. Just like on those notes."

The men wore T-shirts stretched over taut muscles. Denim jeans rode low on their hips. Somebody in their group sighed at the sight.

Margie said, "We'll put them at the bottom of the suspect list for now."

Tootsie said, "You should talk to them, though. They've been here at odd hours and may have seen the person who delivered Father Joe in the rug."

Lily said, "You know who we have to bring into our group now?"

Margie's heart beat faster. "Not Tony."

"No. Felicity," Lily said. "It's a priest hidden under her mansion porch. She's a former nun. Maybe she'll feel some vibe."

Rita said, "We could try her with a Ouija board. It might spell out the killer's name."

Lily Bauer said, "I'm not sure Catholics believe in Ouija board stuff."

Jeri piped in with, "Shouldn't we bring in Deputy Lily Schuster?"

Lily shook her head. "Margie has hidden a corpse."

"Automatic jail time," Tootsie added.

Margie shuddered. "You're scaring me."

Rita nodded. "We all heard about that guy who kept his mother in his freezer. He got bunches of jail time. And she wasn't murdered. Just died in her sleep."

"I didn't murder Father Joe."

Tootsie said, "But it looks like it. A freezer would buy you time to find another priest and have the wedding. Then we could dump the body. The forestland here in northern Wisconsin stretches across counties and is pretty remote. People are known to be lost for days, have heart attacks while hunting and not found until a week later."

To Margie's horror, the women considered the notion. "Stop it. We can't take Father Joe to the woods. We have to solve the murder. He was going to marry me and Tony. I owe him."

For a moment they sipped their coffee in thought.

Lily asked, "So how'd he die? That might lead us to the killer. Was there blood on him?"

"Hard to tell. The rug is mostly red."

Tootsie took a bite of pancake. "We have to move him. We can look for blood then."

Margie shivered. "Why do we have to move him?"

"He's going to start stinking under there. It's supposed to be in the nineties for a week."

Rita offered, "My husband sells garden lime. It kills smells."

Jeri said, "I've got kitty litter we use to cover up puke on the bus."

"All right," Margie said, flinching again. "At least that's a better plan than the freezer."

To their shock, Antoinette walked up to them. "A plan? Might I be of some help?"

Margie thought fast. "We wondered if Aunt Alberta might give a concert in the park in the town square this evening? As a way to introduce your family to Moonstone."

Antoinette hugged Margie. "My Tony will love it. Graci, graci. You bring honor to our family. Now, hurry. We're to meet Father Joe on Tony's boat in ten minutes."

The friends locked gazes and didn't dare move.

"Why?" asked Margie.

"Father Joe will bless the boat and we want to talk about your honeymoon."

Margie wondered what size freezer to get--for Antoinette.

On the tour boat, just west of town, Tony proudly introduced Giovanni Casale to his mother. After Gio left to prepare steak rollups, Antoinette kissed her son on both cheeks.

"My Antonio. This yacht, the fine chef--you have made such stylish choices." She looked at Margie with glistening eyes. "Will he not make a perfect patriarch some day?"

Patriarch. Father. Head of a family? Margie tried to imagine herself as head of the troupe that had taken over the LeBarron mansion. Margie's neck hairs stood up like Herman's when he smelled a skunk. When was Tony going to tell his mother they didn't plan to have children? That Margie just wanted to run her little IGA grocery? Sure, she could technically have eggs hiding out inside of her, and having Tony's baby wouldn't be a bad thing of course, but if she didn't figure out what to do about Father Joe her eggs would fry in jail.

"Excuse me," Margie said, "I'll help Gio while you take the tour."

She found Gio below deck in the galley pounding meat. She empathized with pounding something to get out her frustrations. "Has Antoinette changed the menus on this boat, too?"

"So many changes." He kept pounding, a bit hard, Margie felt.

"Has Tony said anything about his plans? About me?"

"Tony wants to make me head chef."

"If Tony thinks you're ready to be in charge, then you are."

"But if I fail my whole career can be ruined."

Margie impulsively hugged Gio. "Harris hired you originally. Maybe turn the tables. Hire Harris to help you. Take him off my hands."

"Harris would be trouble." But he gave her a thumb's up.

Margie went up to the main deck to rejoin Antoinette but she'd left with Tony, likely in search of Father Joe.

⸺⸺◦❧☙◦⸺⸺

Later, while stocking cabbages Margie found another paper bag, this one with a broken glass elephant. She marched to the register. Harris had been in charge of the store all day.

She shook the bag at him. "What do you need fifty thousand dollars for?"

"Huh?"

"Were you trying to get money so we could elope to Mexico? Did Father Joe catch you leaving your nasty notes? Is that why you killed him?" *Oops. Nincompoop.*

"Father Joe's dead?"

"How did you kill him?"

"I know nothin'." Harris blinked several times. "My gosh, he's dead? How?"

Margie sucked in a calming breath. "You weren't trying to wreck my wedding?"

"Hey, I'm in love with ya, but I wouldn't kill for ya. Is he really dead?"

"I found him this morning. It's why I had you come in early. He's under the porch."

"Oh, man, I want nothin' to do with this. They'll find out about my unpaid parking tickets in college."

"Who'd you see with Father Joe recently?"

"He was with Tony and Gio on the boat, settling some argument."

"Gio just told me. Tony wants him to become head chef."

Harris rearranged paper bags. "Gio and I went bowling last night and he never said a word."

Margie recalled Gio pounding the meat with extra vigor. "I don't think Gio's all that thrilled by the offer."

"When you gonna call Deputy Schuster about Father Joe?"

"I don't know. When I tell her I'll probably go to jail for hiding a corpse."

Margie texted the Moonstone Mavens, minus Felicity, to meet with her at lunchtime to figure out the next step.

She picked up the lime and had just crossed the street in front of the mansion when she saw Herman sniffing at the gate under the front porch. Renzo and Romeo were about to open the latch.

"Renzo! Romeo! Ice cream?"

Squealing, they charged into her legs. She set the lime down behind a rose bush for safekeeping, then led them inside. After steering the boys into the kitchen for ice cream, Margie signaled the Mavens to follow her outside to the gazebo's table, where they'd have privacy. Margie told them about the close call with Herman and the kids.

Lily went wide-eyed. "Herman wouldn't touch Father Joe, would he?"

Rita nodded. "He could drag him out. Our Labrador dragged in a deer carcass yesterday."

Tootsie said, "Venison pot pie is on special today."

"Stop it," Margie said. She told them about the Steuben elephant. "Something bad is about to happen again."

Jeri lifted a bag off the gazebo's wood floor. "Kitty litter. Father Joe's safe from Herman's nose sniffing him out."

Margie said, "I bought lime. It's behind a rose bush."

Having heard his name, Herman padded to them wagging his tail. He dropped a hammer he'd been carrying. Red smudges covered the hammer's head. In shock, the women swung their gazes to the shirtless carpenters working yards away.

Margie's body went heavy as wet cement. "Now what do we do?"

Lily fondled her pearls. "If they're guilty there goes our view."

Rita said, "My husband sells hammers like that. He said Dusty and Casey bought new tools the other day. On credit."

"Because they plan to get fifty-thousand dollars soon," Tootsie said, "from Margie."

Using a napkin, Margie picked up the hammer. "What do we do with it?"

Jeri said, "We can sneak it under the porch when everybody's listening to the opera. We have to sprinkle Father Joe with litter and lime anyway."

Later that evening, as Alberta sang her aria in the park, Margie and her girlfriends went to the storage area under the porch only to find that Father Joe was gone.

Chapter 6

argie searched the property, pretending to take Herman for walks. The dog's sniffer failed to find Father Joe.

After midnight, a few minutes into Thursday, Tony and Margie made love on the sofa in the first floor library. Like a pheromone musk, the heady scent of books excited Tony.

Margie tried to confess everything to him, but the man whispered clichéd metaphors about mountains while smothering her body in kisses. When they rolled onto the floor, Margie happened to glance under the sofa and saw Father Joe behind it.

More sweat popped across her skin.

Tony had seen nothing. He took her face in his hands. "My angel, tell me what you want and I'll get it for you."

"I want to go to bed."

"You vixen."

"No, I mean, to sleep." *To think up a plan.*

"A busy day ahead?"

"I have several errands before the wedding." *I have to get rid of a body.*

Margie lay awake trying to figure out who could've moved the body and why. Dustin and Casey could be trying to pin the murder on Tony's family. Those carpenters--if that's who they really were--could leave the state or country before Deputy Lily Schuster knew anything. Margie couldn't bear Tony and his family taking the blame.

Intent on moving Father Joe out of the mansion, she got out of bed at around five a.m. and sneaked to the first floor. A shuffling from inside the library made her freeze. The door opened. "Antoinette?"

The woman, dressed in a creamy nightgown, dropped Father Joe. She'd obviously been dragging him by his shoulders. His head smacked loudly enough to panic both of them. "Now look what you've done."

"What are you doing?" Margie whispered.

"Getting him out of this house to save Tony. Why did you put Father Joe under the porch? To blame Tony?"

"You automatically blamed me?" Margie's hands formed fists at her sides.

"I asked Nico if he'd done it and he said 'no'. No others in my family would do such a thing and be able to keep it a secret."

"Maybe Nico lied. Maybe he accidentally karate-chopped Father Joe to death."

A door opened and shut on the second floor. "Hurry," Antoinette said.

In seconds, Margie and Antoinette hid the dead priest behind the library's sofa again. Margie flopped onto the sofa to catch her breath. Antoinette sat in a chair.

Margie asked, "Why did you bring the body to the library?"

"Nobody reads today. Nobody will come in here."

That made Margie giggle. The situation was so absurd. Antoinette smiled, too. Margie was forced to say, "The murder investigation is going to involve your whole family. Nico seems to have a bad past. The wedding...will have to be canceled."

"Indeed not." Antoinette pulled up the sleeves of her satin nightgown. "What if Nico is telling the truth?"

"Then who did it?"

"Do you have a computer?"

"Across the hall in the den."

Antoinette got up and strode to the door. "You and I shall research Father Joe."

Margie chastised herself for not doing that earlier.

Chapter 7

argie and Antoinette found only ordinary stuff about Father Joe serving Illinois parishes before they heard several voices in the hallway and had to shut down the computer. They rushed to sit on the sofa that hid Father Joe.

Nobody came in, to their relief.

With the search a dead-end for now, Antoinette asked about the hammer, which she'd hidden behind a book in the library. "If the carpenters did it, why did they ask for fifty-thousand dollars *specifically*?"

Margie peered at the woman in a new way. "Maybe that's what a new truck costs." Margie rose. "It's time I tell the deputy."

"Certainly we can wait until after Tony's wedding--"

"It's off, Antoinette."

"But I found a supplier of white doves."

"The hawks around here would've eaten the doves."

With her queen-like demeanor, Antoinette swished out of the den.

Minutes later, miserable, Margie opened her IGA store. She had to put her thoughts in order before seeing the deputy, and then of course, Tony. In all likelihood, she, Nico, maybe Dusty and Casey would end up behind bars before sunset. The bloody hammer had to have come from the carpenters, Margie felt.

She busied herself waiting for Harris. He didn't show. He was always prompt. She called him a couple of times to no avail.

With a creepy chill clutching her she searched the store. She found a bag with a broken Steuben horse. This note said: *Money. Now. Second murder.*

Second? Who? Her brain connected money, the mansion, Father Joe, and the Steubens and out popped the name of Henri LeBarron. If the murderer killed one old man, would Henri be the next elderly man to die? Henri was rich. Certainly threatening him could yield fifty thousand dollars.

Minutes later, she knocked on her trailer's door. Felicity stepped outside in her bathrobe. "What's wrong?"

"Henri's in danger."

"How?"

"I should've told you all this before and I'm sorry I didn't trust you..." Margie related everything, then added, "You knew Father Joe when you were studying to be a nun in Illinois. What are we missing? Why does somebody want fifty thousand dollars from me?"

Felicity's face went slack. "Harris."

"Harris?"

"He asked me about Father Joe's past."

"What'd you tell him?"

"I knew *of* Father Joe but I didn't really know him. But Harris seemed upset."

Margie's heart ached. Harris killed Father Joe? If he didn't, what was Harris up to?

Felicity said, "Hold on." She took out her cell phone and placed a call to a friend in Illinois. After the call, she looked stunned. "Harris has been calling around, trying to find dirt on Father Joe."

"Is there any?"

"Apparently Harris was an altar boy at one of Father Joe's parishes."

"You mean--?"

Felicity shook her head. "But Father Joe served on a committee that looked at cases of abuse. Maybe there's some connection."

"Harris had a grudge against the Father?" Her stomach threatened to rebel. "But why would Harris ask *me* for money?"

Realization snapped in Felicity's dark eyes. "We moved out of the mansion so fast that I'm betting the note was meant for Henri to find, not you."

That made sense to Margie. "I'm so sorry. Then the notes kept coming to me because they figured I was marrying into a rich family, too."

While Margie paused to think through what she knew so far, Felicity asked, "Do you think it could be Dusty and Casey? I mean, the hammer seems like a direct connection."

"Yes, there is that possible connection." She mentioned Harris disappearing, though.

"Is there any connection between Harris and the carpenters?"

Margie couldn't fathom Harris murdering anybody, but he had big bills to pay off yet for college loans. Then there was crazy Nico, and Antoinette possibly covering up for him. Harris and Gio were close friends, so it could mean that Gio was in on this, too. Could it be that Gio and Harris had acted together? At the very least, maybe Gio was covering for Harris? Or was it the other way around?

Margie's head throbbed. "Lock the doors. I might know who killed Father Joe."

Chapter 8

At Deputy Lily Schuster's office Margie unloaded everything she knew.

The deputy was aghast at Margie's tale, but said she'd of course make inquiries and send an ambulance and officials to collect the body. The deputy asked Margie to not say anything. Instead, Margie was to say only that Father Joe was found in the library but cause of death was to be determined.

The deputy further wanted Margie to collect any information she could about any odd behavior or information she might find around the mansion or on the tour boat where Father Joe might have been. The deputy surmised the priest may have been killed on the boat, then transferred to the mansion's front steps.

***

Margie hurried back to the mansion, eager to talk again with Antoinette because the woman had found Father Joe and had been trying to move him.

Was she trying to protect the killer? Margie thought it possible. Nico was still a prime suspect.

The mansion hummed with Farinas getting ready for a trip to Tootsie's chicken farm. Antoinette was upstairs, Kirsten said. Kirsten was experimenting with a luscious Italian breakfast bakery item made with ruby chocolate for the early morning breakfast following the wedding day. Obviously Antoinette hadn't said a word about the canceled wedding.

Domenico held court with his grown children in the Jingle Bell Inn. The family picture tugged at Margie's heart. She ducked into the hallway leading to the mansion proper.

"Look what we found!" Renzo announced.

Romeo and Renzo stood on either side of Herman. The dog was dragging Father Joe by his shirt along the floor. Margie almost wet her pants.

"Kids, uh, Father Joe took some medicine and isn't feeling well. You get ice cream while I help him back to the library sofa, okay?" She handed them dollar bills and they took off.

Used to carrying heavy sacks in her store, Margie got Father Joe back to the library within seconds. She shut the door.

To be safe, she ushered nosey Herman out the front door, noticing the Farinas were boarding the bus for the outing.

She went into the library. This time, with a better hunch about things, she searched for Dusty and Casey, and Harris. Without Antoinette lurking about, she felt freer to do more extensive searches.

Then bingo. She found juicy tidbits. It shocked her but confirmed what Felicity said about Harris asking questions. As teenagers the men had been arrested for petty theft. The three men--Dusty, Casey, and Harris--knew each other in the past.

Margie left the den to see if the carpenters were outside working on the gazebo. Indeed, they were. She took a deep breath. Confronting them could be dangerous, but she was a good screamer, so ventured outside.

After rushing up to them, she had to momentarily pause because they had shed their shirts again on the hot summer day. Their bronzed, muscular chests and biceps gleamed under the sun.

She addressed Dusty first, only because he winked at her, his gray-blue eyes almost paralyzing her with their beauty. "Dusty, I'm looking for Harris. Do you know where he went?"

Dusty shook his head, then turned to Casey next to him who was leaning over a spade. "Case, you seen anything of Harris?"

Casey shrugged, then shook his head. "Isn't he helping that chef get ready for your wedding next week? He must have a lot of errands to run."

Margie tried glowering at them. "Where is he? I know that you two know him. From years ago. Does shoplifting ring a bell?"

Casey jerked to attention, leaning over his spade handle. "Where'd you hear that?"

"You certainly didn't change your names after the shoplifting arrest and the internet is quite helpful digging up dirt on people."

The two men exchanged a glance.

Margie said, "Which one of you is missing a hammer?"

Dusty's eyes went wider. "You found it? Where? That dog take it?"

"He did, but there's the matter of the blood on it." Margie was shaking now. She backed off for safety's sake. "Which one of you clobbered Father Joe over the head with it?"

Both men gasped. Casey dropped the spade. It clunked against the sawhorse nearby. He said, "We didn't do anything. We don't know anything about Father Joe."

They appeared genuinely scared, but she suspected they were lying.

Margie's mouth went dry. She could barely form words. "Did Harris kill Father Joe? Is Harris on the run? Is that why I haven't been able to find him? Why he didn't come to work?"

Casey picked up his spade, then exchanged a look with his buddy. "We have to tell her."

"Tell me what?" Margie asked.

"Harris. He, well, Harris told us once he'd testified at some priest's trial many years ago. He didn't name names, though. Harris always sounded bitter."

"How bitter?"

This Dusty said, "He said he had wanted to kill somebody he was so mad about the outcome. He told us those trials cost a lot of money, thousands. He kept saying he just wanted what was due him."

Margie went back inside, thinking Dusty and Casey knew a lot they weren't telling. She called Deputy Schuster.

She went back to the library where Father Joe was in repose, then sat at the computer desk to key in "fifty thousand dollars" along with the words "priest" and "abuse". Up popped Harris's name again. And Tony's! Harris and Tony had testified at a hearing about priests a few years ago, on opposite sides. Harris's side had lost the trial, to the tune of fifty thousand dollars in lawyer's fees. Margie had to sit back and consider that. Was Harris a murderer now? Getting some kind of revenge because he disagreed with the outcome of a hearing? Did Tony suspect Harris--the man who wanted to run away with her was covering up something?

The name of the juvenile boy alleging the abuse wasn't mentioned of course. But Margie had a hunch who that might be. She knew names of the children weren't allowed to be known in hearings and court cases, at least years ago. Tony couldn't know the name. But what about Harris? And Dusty and Casey? Gossip never rested; it was like a hummingbird flitting from flower to flower, or reaching one person and another.

Margie rushed outside. Out front of the mansion the bus with the family seemed to have been delayed but was now leaving. Margie saw the county sheriff's vehicle moving along the street further down the way, coming toward them.

She rushed inside to find Antoinette. Margie wanted to ask the older woman about Tony's involvement in that Illinois hearing, though Margie doubted Tony would have told her mother about an awful episode involving a priest. Tony seemed to want to spare the women in his life from anything not pleasant. Tony wanted happiness. Somehow, the thought made Margie even more eager to solve this case, maybe to protect Tony. She wanted to protect kindness in the world.

Kirsten rushed from the kitchen, her eyes wide. "Lily Schuster just arrested Casey and Dusty for murder."

Margie swallowed the lump in her throat. "I had them arrested."

"They really did it? With the hammer?"

"I don't think so. But they know some details, and being arrested keeps them safe and will shake loose what they know. Where's Antoinette?"

"She went out to the cruise boat."

"Oh no." When Margie was doing her research on the Web she'd noticed one of the links had been colored purple, not blue. Purple denoted that somebody had opened that same website. "Tell Deputy Schuster that Antoinette is in danger. I have to run."

"Why? What's going on, Margie?"

"Harris and Gio are in the middle of some grudge match. That's why I couldn't get reach or find Harris earlier. Hurry!"

"Are they the ones with the ransom notes? Did they kill Father Joe?"

"One of them did."

Chapter 9

At the dock, Margie saw the big cruise boat already motoring away. She looked at the small fishing boats for rent. But the old geezer who rented them, Oscar Parsons, was nowhere around. Margie was probably responsible for his murder now, too. Angry with herself for being so hesitant lately about everything in her life, she changed in that instant and became bold. She leaped into one of the fishing boats.

While the big cruise boat puttered slowly to get away from shore, the smaller fishing boat could skim across the surface of the cove much faster. Within minutes Margie maneuvered alongside the cruise boat, tied up, then climbed up the ladder--with caution.

Finding nobody around, she slithered across the deck, then entered the party cabin.

Antoinette's voice emanated from the galley below deck. Margie tiptoed closer to the stairwell, scared. She overheard Antoinette say, "Because of you the wedding's off. My Tony is ruined. Are you satisfied?"

"Not until you're dead."

Margie gasped out loud. Gio rushed up the stairs, stepped around the corner and yanked Margie by the hair, hauling her down to the galley. He held a large butcher knife at her throat.

Antoinette yelled, "Giovanni, let her go."

Tony's mother was bound to a chair by two aprons and their sashes. Margie's heart banged like pan lids. "Gio, what are you doing? Where's Harris?"

Gio shoved Margie at Antoinette. "I want what's owed me. One of you is going to get the money for me, then we set sail for Canada."

Antoinette cried out, "Gio murdered Father Joe."

Margie trembled behind Antoinette. "I know. I found the website you'd been on. Gio, Father Joe only served on the panel that looked into the abuse. He never abused you. Why did you kill Father Joe?"

Gio exchanged the knife for a huge cleaver. "Father Joe recommended that pervert be moved across the country to another parish."

"That was long ago, Gio, and I'm sorry for you. It could be that Father Joe was pressured. After all, he was sent away from that place and came here to work. Father Joe likely suffered a lot because he was silenced. And don't you realize you can still bring charges? A lawyer can help you."

"Hah. Lawyers cost money and it would take years to find that priest and bring him to justice."

Margie could see there was no consoling Giovanni Casale. He'd killed Father Joe, after all. "What did you do with Harris?"

Gio laughed, shaking the meat cleaver.

Margie tried again. "Your money won't magically pop out of people's graves."

Antoinette stirred. "Such a big man you are, Giovanni, preying on my family, trying to pin a murder on us, extorting money. I spit on you."

To Margie's shock, Antoinette spit at the man.

Gio threw the cleaver.

Margie leaped aside, screaming. The cleaver sank into the maple pantry door behind her. Items tumbled about, making a racket.

Gio grabbed the meat mallet.

Margie yelled, "Gio, Harris wouldn't like this!"

"Harris is weak."

"Harris was called to testify at that trial for the priest. So was Tony."

Antoinette shrieked, "My Tony?"

Margie said, "He didn't tell me, either, because Tony doesn't dwell on bad things or the past. But Tony never saw any abuse and neither did Harris, which made your case fall apart. Harris was mad about the whole thing, too. Right, Gio?" She stared at the mallet. "Harris was your friend, but he had to tell the truth. And the other day, just like I did, Harris noticed how you left my store in a hurry to avoid Father Joe. Harris started asking you questions about the missing priest, didn't he? He called around in Illinois, hoping to find out that anybody but you would have a grudge against Father Joe. Harris didn't like what went on either. It cost a lot of money--maybe fifty thousand dollars in lawyer fees--and nothing came of it. Right? Were you abused?"

Gio laughed. "Me? No. My friends were."

"What have you done with your friend Harris?"

Gio smacked the mallet into his palm. "The fish have to eat."

Margie's heartbeat skittered. Was Harris really dead? "And if Tony had stayed on the boat today, you'd have killed him, too?"

The chef's smile made Margie leap to the counter for a frying pan. "Come on, Gio. Me and you."

The boat tipped on a wave. The contents in the closet behind her tumbled again. How odd not to have things secured on a boat, unless...

Gio stepped toward her. Margie flung her pan at him, but tripped backward and hit her head on the pantry door. She lay stunned, eyes closed. She sensed Gio walking over to her. Then he went back to Antoinette. "Let's feed the fish a gourmet dish."

Antoinette said, "She called the police. Run. I'll send you money."

While Gio chortled over that, Margie heard noises in the pantry again. It couldn't be Harris. Then she smiled with a lot of hope. She waited until Gio was sliding Antoinette toward the door. She jumped up and opened the pantry door. "Get him, Herman!"

The giant Saint Bernard leaped at Gio, toppling him over Antoinette. Margie whacked the young chef over the head with the pan. He dropped with a grunt.

Antoinette groaned from the floor. "I've broken my arm."

Margie untied her and got her up. "But you're alive. Smart of you to bring Herman along."

"He followed me. I'm not smart at all."

"I beg to differ, except for spitting on the guy with the knife."

Within a minute, Margie had Gio tied tighter than a rolled roast. She hurried up to the deck with Herman to find Harris and Oscar. When Herman barked ferociously she discovered a dark speck way out in the lake.

"Harris!" She doubted he could hear her. But the deputy was already motoring into the lake and followed Margie's directions.

Margie managed a shaky trip piloting the boat back against the dock. She helped Antoinette ashore, then hurried to hug Harris and Oscar as they arrived. Harris had dived into the lake to save Oscar when Gio knocked him overboard.

Jeri pulled in with the busload of Farinas. The Mavens' cars screeched in beside the bus. Domenico hustled to Antoinette.

Tony hugged Margie. "My Sophia Loren, are you all right?"

With the life-threatening tension gone, Margie crumpled. "The wedding's off."

He took her face in his hands. "What is it you want? I will give it to you."

The Moonstone Mavens crowded around. Lily said, "You're getting married. We won't let you go to jail."

Tony gasped with shock. "Jail?"

All energy drained from Margie. "You're the sweetest man I know, but Tony, it just won't work. I've been part of some horrible things."

Tony kissed her hand. "I'll go to prison for you. But what is this about?"

"I hid a body and didn't tell you. I did a lot of things and didn't tell you. I...didn't trust you." Maybe he hadn't told her everything, but she was just as guilty. "The lack of trust isn't a good way to start a marriage."

He got down on his knees. "I want to marry you."

The Mavens' heads bobbed. "Where else can we wear those poufy pink dresses?"

Margie looked at all her girlfriends, then down at Tony. "You're all so nice. And that's the problem. Because you were trying to help me, I hesitated going to the deputy. I also lied, and I almost blamed innocent people." She nodded toward Antoinette and Nico. "Even Antoinette has been trying to be nice, helping me with her advice. But I didn't speak up, or stand up for myself. With any of you."

She sucked in a fortifying breath. "I'm confused. I don't want to be confused anymore. I want to be me. Whatever that is. And I'm going to go find out what that is. Because Harris is taking me to Mexico."

"What?!" the crowd yelped.

Chapter 10

Later that Thursday afternoon Dusty and Casey were freed. Gio confessed to using their hammer to murder Father Joe and to stealing the Steubens.

Margie moved back to her trailer. Felicity and her family returned to the mansion. That night, after dark, while she packed, Tony showed up at her door. Again.

"Tony, it won't work between us."

"You're wrong, but I also respect that you need to think about things."

"You do?" Her heart fluttered toward him like a moth to her porch light. She batted at one flitting about her face.

"Yes. I thought I'd wish you *bon voyage* by making love to you on the roof of your trailer. Under the stars."

Tony began unbuttoning his white shirt.

Margie gulped. "I wish I could say I'll get the ladder."

Tony's eyes dimmed in the dark night. Margie expected Tony to take her face in his hands, look inside her soul and tell her the usual things about loving her and all her sexy parts. But he merely backed away, then left. It was as if he were giving her exactly what she expected to have happen: a cancelled wedding.

By late Friday afternoon, she and Harris were at a resort south of Cancun on the Gulf of Mexico. Years ago, in a dreamy phase, she'd gotten a passport, but she'd never had the courage to actually use it. Now, she was tasting the thrill of being somebody she'd never been before. Brave? Full of gumption?

They had separate rooms, but Harris insisted they share a bottle of wine on her balcony overlooking the ocean. The only shore she'd seen in her entire life was Lake Superior's. The salt spray on the breeze tickled her cheek; it reminded her of Tony's touch. She watched people parasailing and drifting over the azure water; she just might try that. Children squealed, interrupting the peace. Two boys that looked like Renzo and Romeo from a distance built a sandcastle. A prick of homesickness hit her.

Had she really jilted Tony? She'd get over him. After all, he'd told Father Joe she was strong. He'd also told Father Joe she'd make a good mother. It still made her steam. She'd been a chump not to speak up. She'd been hoodwinked by all the "nice". She realized now that it wasn't the idea of having children that bothered her; it was that everybody assumed she and Tony would have some, even Tony hadn't really listened to her. He was too intent upon worshipping her with all of his kisses.

She missed his kisses, but she had to move forward. There would be another beau.

Harris suggested they go to bed early. He had plans tomorrow for a trip to some Mayan ruin, and a fishing excursion--things to make her forget the past horrid week.

On Saturday morning she dressed in a gift Harris had left at her door--crisp white clam digger pants with a white lacy caftan top that fit over a silk camisole-style blouse. She wished Antoinette could see the duds.

When she went down to the dining room, she found the double doors locked. She looked again at the ticket. This was the right room for the brunch buffet.

One door cracked open. Harris popped out, his face red, as if from exertion. "You are lovely enough to eat."

"What's going on?"

Harris opened the doors. Margie nearly fainted. The Farinas and the Moonstone Mavens stared back.

"So those boys on the beach *were* Renzo and Romeo."

Harris winked. "It was all I could do to keep you in your room so that they could get the wedding ready."

"Wedding? I told everyone that..."

She noticed the tables and chairs had been moved so that an aisle led to where Tony appeared at the front of the room in a white suit with a pink shirt.

Suddenly she woke up; everybody wore pink, even Antoinette, with a pink-brimmed hat to boot. Antoinette had dressed in Margie's favorite color!

Margie didn't know what to do; she started to back up.

Renzo and Romeo rushed to give her a leg hug. Romeo clutched a pink, satin pillow with wedding bands tied on top. "Uncle Tony thaid we're thuppothed to walk ahead of you."

Her girlfriends took their places near Tony. The ocean roared through the open, sliding glass doors. The Farina brothers, all wearing pink shirts, took their places by Tony. The color pink began to swim in Margie's eyes.

Someone handed her a hankie. "My dear, you look lovely. But not lovely enough."

Antoinette held Margie's wedding dress across her arms, one in a cast. The pink sash encircled the waist.

Margie let anger bubble up. "Was all this your idea?"

"No."

Tony trotted down the aisle. "It was mine. I had to try one last time to make you see we're meant to be together."

He snatched the wedding gown from his mother, grabbed Margie by the hand, then steered them down the hall and into an office.

"Tony, you can't just expect me to marry you."

"Why not?"

"Because--"

"Of my mother?" He held the gown reverently in front of him.

"Yes. She wants us to have children and you went along with it instead of supporting me. Instead of asking me."

"What?!"

"Father Joe told me. He said you told him I was strong and would make a good mother."

"Father Joe was hard of hearing. I said you were a good woman like my mother, but you were strong enough not to let the hints about children get to you."

Margie swallowed. "Oh, dear. Really?"

He nodded.

"But what about your building a villa for us like your family's villa? Your father expects you to do for me what he did for your mother."

Tony laid the dress over a nearby chair then took her hands. "Honey, I need to tell you something I found out about my mother that I found out from my dad. She's never told anyone this."

He scared her a little. "Then don't tell me."

"I have to. The fertility rug was a gift from my father to my mother."

Oh here we go. She gave Tony a disappointed look.

He patted her hands. "On a walk the other night, my father told me they lost two babies before I was born. I'm not the eldest brother."

She touched his face. "I'm so sorry."

"After their deaths, my father said my mother was inconsolable. He bought the rug and had it blessed. My father told my mother that if she would dance with him each night on the rug, good things would come of their love. In nine months I came along."

Margie took his face in her hands. "That's a beautiful story. You broke the jinx."

Tony's dark eyes shimmered. "She dotes on all of us without meaning any harm, Margie."

"But what about you, Tony? Do you want to have children after all?"

"Only the two of us vote on that one, not my mother or anybody else. Besides, have you heard the way Renzo and Romeo screech? I can't take that after a day of noise on party boats. I want to come home to you and the peace of the trailer."

Margie fell into his arms.

"I think it's time we undress you."

"Tony?!"

"So you can put on that wedding dress. My mother hand-sewed the pink sash and bow back on it herself during the plane ride. Despite the cast on her arm."

Margie giggled. "She...means well. She loves large. And I like her for that."

Minutes later, Tony and Margie stood on the fertility rug at the front of the room and were married.

Antoinette and the Moonstone Mavens created the most beautiful wedding reception the resort had ever seen. Antoinette had made sure the antique gelatin molds came along. A dozen wiggly gelatin bunnies, bears, and fish decorated with strawberry slices and marshmallows were a hit.

After the cutting of the cake, Tony took Margie's face between his hands. "My angel, what is it you want the most in life? I'll give it to you."

"Tony Farina, I want to grow old with you."

While he kissed her, applause erupted.

Margie walked over to Antoinette and Dom, handed each a champagne glass, then faced the crowd. "Ladies and gentlemen, meet my new mother and father. I'm proud to say I'm a Farina."

Aunt Alberta took that as her cue and hit a sopranic high note, shattering the glass held in Antoinette's hand. Champagne sprayed her pink silk dress. Antoinette's face clouded.

The family held its breath.

Then the matriarch started laughing. And everybody else did, too.

She whispered to Margie, "Serves me right. From now on, stop me from my foolish mistakes. She sings off-key but I've never had the guts to tell her. If only I could have your courage to speak up."

Margie gave her a hug.

The Farinas left the resort on Monday. Harris and the women friends left soon after. Tony and Margie stayed for two weeks.

Then they settled into their pink trailer with Herman. Curiously, though, when school started that fall, Margie noticed Moonstone was quiet in a way she hadn't noticed before.

One evening she said to Tony, "Herman misses Renzo and Romeo. Do you think we could invite them here this coming Christmas?"

Tony asked, "*Herman* misses the boys?"

She smiled. "Yes. *Herman* does."

"Well, for Herman then. We'll take Herman and our nephews sledding, skating, and skiing--"

She smothered Tony in kisses, took his face in her hands and asked, "What is it you want, Antonio, my love? I'll give it to you."

That led to Tony's favorite activity that also started with an "S".

THE END

If you enjoyed this author's book, then please place a review up at the site of purchase, and any social media sites you frequent!

You can find ALL our books on our website at:

http://www.writers-exchange.com

All our romances:

http://www.writers-exchange.com/category/genres/romance/

All Christine's Books:

http://www.writers-exchange.com/christine-desmet/

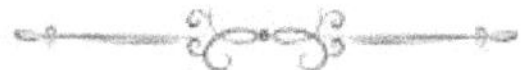

About the Author

Christine **DeSmet** is an award-winning fiction writer and professional screenwriter. She is the author of the bestselling *Fudge Shop Mystery Series* and the popular novella series called *Mischief in Moonstone.*

She is a Distinguished Faculty Associate in Writing at University of Wisconsin-Madison where she teaches novel writing and screenwriting and directs the annual summer Write-by-the-Lake Writer's Workshop & Retreat. Through her master classes she has seen many of her adult students become published.

She is also a professional writing coach in the UW-Madison Writers' Institute conference's Pathway to Publication program.

Christine is a member of Mystery Writers of America, Sisters in Crime, Wisconsin Writers Association, Wisconsin Screenwriters Association, and other professional associations.

Christine is active on Facebook and you can also find her at http://www.ChristineDeSmet.com

Christine's author page at Writers Exchange E-Publishing is: http://www.writers-exchange.com/christine-desmet/

If you want to read more about books by this author, they are listed on the following pages...

Fudge Shop Mystery Series

Deadly Fudge Divas

A taste of trouble is in the air when a group of well-heeled, fudge-loving women descend on Ava Oosterling's newly acquired and lovingly refurbished bed & breakfast inn for a chocolate lovers' getaway.

When one of the women turns up dead--and Ava's grandfather is a prime suspect--Ava plunges into the thick of a murder case stickier than her candy store's line of Fairy Tale fudge flavors and the chocolate facials the women adore at the local spa.

It's springtime and the start of the tourist season in Fishers' Harbor, Wisconsin. Ava has opened the Blue Heron Inn with the help of handsome construction worker Dillon Rivers. Unfortunately, Dillon's mother--Ava's ex-mother-in-law--is among the secretive divas who become suspects along with Grandpa.

Ava turns for help from her friends but they have troubles, too. One is eager for a wedding proposal to unfold on live television, while another friend is expecting her first baby and asks Ava to assist with the birth.

Everything and everybody Ava loves seems in chaos--her fudge shop, her inn, her family, and her own friendships... Until she uncovers a thirty-year-old secret of the "deadly fudge divas".
Publisher: https://www.writers-exchange.com/deadly-fudge-divas/

Undercover Fudge

Candy shop owner Ava Oosterling has her hands full when her best friend Pauline Mertens takes a summer job as a wedding coordinator--with the nuptials and reception scheduled in mere days in the back yard of Ava's Blue Heron Inn overlooking Lake Michigan's bay.

To help out her best friend, Ava is intent on making the table favors-- edible fudge lighthouses patterned after their county's 11 lighthouses.

Unfortunately, trying to finish the luscious ruby chocolate lighthouses becomes elusive. The sheriff informs Ava that a band of thieves storming the country may have targeted this wedding. And that's because there's proof Pauline's mother is associated with the thieves.

When the sheriff asks Ava to go undercover, she finds herself in an emotional quagmire. Pauline's mother only recently returned to Fishers' Harbor after years of estrangement from her daughter. And, Coletta Mertens now works as the housekeeper at Ava's inn. Has Ava's fudge-and-wine hospitality provided a hideout for a criminal?

Unfortunately, "until death do us part" takes a murderous twist involving Ava's Grandpa Gil, the dog Lucky Harbor, and Ava's own beau.

Publisher: https://www.writers-exchange.com/undercover-fudge/

Holly Jolly Fudge Folly

An early, deep snow has gifted Fishers' Harbor, Wisconsin, with a perfect setting for the holiday celebration. Unfortunately removing snow from Main Street for the parade reveals the dead tax assessor with a knife in him-- containing Grandpa Gil's fingerprints.

It's clearly a setup and one that keeps Ava and Grandpa Gil under the watchful eyes of Sheriff Tollefson. Who wants Grandpa to miss playing Santa Claus in the Christmas parade and why? Who's being naughty instead of nice?

Grandpa doesn't help his case with talk of leaving town for good--words that chill Ava worse than the weather. She can't imagine life without Grandpa's warm hugs and laughter.

When vandals strike the historic shop and someone leaves Ava and fiancé Dillon Rivers for dead in the snow, Ava wonders if she may need the magical help of Santa's elves to solve the holiday folly.

Publisher: https://www.writers-exchange.com/holly-jolly-fudge-folly/

Mischief in Moonstone Series

Nestled against the sparkling shores of Lake Superior, the tiny village of Moonstone is anything but ordinary. Between romantic entanglements, quirky neighbors, and mysteries that seem to pop up with every season, the locals know life here comes with a generous dose of laughter and surprise. From silkie chickens and a giant prehistoric beaver skeleton to kidnapped reindeer and holiday hijinks, mischief is always waiting just around the corner. Fall in love with the humorous, heartwarming adventures of Moonstone--where romance meets mayhem in the most delightful ways.

Novella 1: When Rudolf was Kidnapped

Crystal Hagan's first-graders are in panic mode. Their beloved holiday reindeer, Rudolph, has been stolen from the school's live Christmas display. Without him, the children are convinced Christmas is canceled.

The trail of mischief leads to Peter LeBarron, the wealthy recluse who lives in a mansion locals call the "North Pole." To Crystal's shock, Peter freely admits to taking Rudolph--but he refuses to give him back without some romantic negotiations of his own.

With the holiday countdown ticking, Crystal must juggle her students' worries, a stolen reindeer, and an unexpected suitor who may have just stolen her heart.

Humorous, heartwarming, and filled with small-town Christmas magic, this novella is perfect for fans of cozy romance and holiday cheer.

Publisher: https://www.writers-exchange.com/when-rudolph-was-kidnapped/

Novella 2: Misbehavin' in Moonstone

Kirsten Peplinski has worked hard to open her dream restaurant on the shores of Lake Superior. But when the men of Moonstone start disappearing in the evenings--and her business suffers--she discovers the shocking reason: a touring boat offering topless entertainment just outside town limits.

Determined to put an end to the mischief, Kirsten confronts the boat's infuriatingly handsome owner, Jonathon VanBrocklin. Instead of backing down, Jonathon kidnaps her--claiming undressing and marriage are the only items on his menu.

Caught between outrage and unexpected attraction, Kirsten faces the wildest adventure of her life. Will she escape this reckless scheme, or discover that true love sometimes arrives in the most mischievous packages?

Humorous, romantic, and funny, cheeky, and charming, *Misbehavin' in Moonstone* is a sizzling small-town escape.

Publisher: https://www.writers-exchange.com/misbehavin-in-moonstone/

Novella 3: Mrs. Claus and the Moonstone Murder

New county deputy Lily Schuster is still learning the ropes when trouble strikes in Moonstone, Wisconsin. On her second day, she arrests archaeologist Marcus Linden for trespassing--only to find herself turning to him for help when a pie contest judge ends up murdered.

The suspects? None other than Henri LeBarron, the town's beloved eighty-four-year-old Santa, and his scandalous new companion, the alluring Felicity Starr. Both women are vying to become "Mrs. Claus" for the upcoming winter celebration--and their rivalry has turned deadly.

With August heat bearing down and tempers flaring, Lily must solve the case, keep her wits about her, and decide if Marcus's kisses are worth more than his alibis.

Quirky, romantic, and full of small-town mischief, *Mrs. Claus and the Moonstone Murder* blends mystery with a heart-stealing romance.

Publisher: https://www.writers-exchange.com/mrs-claus-and-the-moonstone-murder/

Novella 4: When the Dead People Brought a Dish-to-Pass

Three days before Halloween, Alyssa Swain finds a dead man in his car. But when she returns with help, the body has vanished.

Things only get stranger when the supposed corpse--scruffy, tall John Christopherson--appears on her doorstep very much alive...or at least claiming to be. John insists she summoned him to help prepare for a Halloween party, and he refuses to leave her house--or her heart.

But midnight on Halloween looms, and Alyssa must find a way to keep John from crossing into the afterlife forever.

Funny, eerie, and tender, When the Dead People Brought a Dish-to-Pass is a paranormal romance that blends small-town charm with Halloween magic.

Publisher: https://www.writers-exchange.com/when-the-dead-people-brought-a-dish-to-pass/

Novella 5: A Moonstone Wedding

Margie Mueller thought wedding jitters were normal--until her fiancé sent her a fertility rug.

She's no spring chicken, and the idea of raising a brood of Farina babies makes her panic. But before she can call the whole thing off, Tony's boisterous family descends on Moonstone with their parties, opinions, and endless interference.

Then a dead man turns up--wrapped in that same fertility rug. Suddenly, Margie's wedding isn't just in danger of collapsing under family chaos--it's at the center of a murder mystery. And Tony may know more than he's admitting.

Funny, quirky, and laced with small-town mischief, A Moonstone Wedding is a romantic novella with a deadly twist.

Publisher: https://www.writers-exchange.com/a-moonstone-wedding/

Novella 6: The Moonstone Fire

John "Bozeman" Hall has seen it all--longhorn cattle, grizzly hunts, even rattlesnake suppers. But nothing prepares him for Moonstone, Wisconsin.

When a suspicious fire destroys the newlyweds Crystal and Peter LeBarron's farm cabin, Bozeman is determined to track down the arsonist. His first suspect? A young homeless mother and her son, squatting in a cave on the property.

But the closer he gets to the truth, the more Bozeman discovers that danger isn't the only spark in town--so is the pull of unexpected love.

The Moonstone Fire delivers a sizzling blend of small-town mystery, heartwarming romance, and the quirky mischief Moonstone is known for.

Publisher: https://www.writers-exchange.com/the-moonstone-fire/

Coming November 2025...

Novella 7: All She Wore Was a Bow

Kincaid Hunter, professional bull rider and decorated veteran, has never been tamed--least of all by the thought of marriage. But when a good friend back home in Wisconsin plans a Christmas wedding, Kincaid can't resist riding in to try and stop him from making what he thinks is a big mistake.

What Kincaid doesn't expect is to be lassoed himself--by a wedding planner dressed as Mrs. Claus, with a sparkle in her eyes and a bow for every occasion.

Soon, the cowboy who vowed he'd never walk down the aisle discovers that love can tie a knot tighter than any rope.

All She Wore Was a Bow is a festive small-town romance full of humor, heart, and holiday magic.

Publisher: https://www.writers-exchange.com/the-moonstone-fire/

Coming Soon:

Novella 8: Pest Control

Novella 9: The Big Love & Murder Shilly-Shally in Moonstone

You can find ALL our books up on our website at:

http://www.writers-exchange.com

All our romances:

http://www.writers-exchange.com/category/genres/romance/

All Christine's Books:

http://www.writers-exchange.com/christine-desmet/

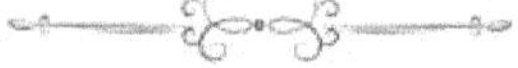